Could You Be an ANGEL Today?

Could You Be an ANGEL Today?

CHRISTINE THACKERAY

CFI
SPRINGVILLE, UTAH

ISBN 13: 978-1-59955-346-7

Published by CFI, an imprint of Cedar Fort, Inc.
2373 W. 700 S., Springville, UT 84663
Distributed by Cedar Fort, Inc., www.cedarfort.com

LIBRARY OF CONGRESS CATALOGING-IN-PUBLICATION DATA

Thackeray, Christine.
  Could you be an angel today? / Christine Thackeray.
    p. cm.
  Poem.
  Summary: The poet trades places with an angel for a day.
  ISBN 978-1-59955-346-7
  1. Service (Theology)--Poetry. 2. Christian poetry, American. I. Title.
  PS3620.H33C68 2010
  811'.6--dc22
                                        2009043197

Cover design and typesetting by Megan Whittier
Cover design © 2010 by Lyle Mortimer
Edited by Melissa J. Caldwell

Printed in the United States of America

10 9 8 7 6 5 4 3 2 1

Printed on acid-free paper

One night, I was sleeping. It'd been a good day.
 The laundry was done and all put away.
The kitchen was spotless; the floor shined like new.
 Tomorrow I hoped there'd be little to do.

S uddenly, in the dark folds of night,
My dreaming was shattered by an angel of light.
His stark white robes glistened. I shielded my eyes.
He cleared his throat and said, "I apologize.

"Your neighborhood angel, a Gladys by name,
Is truly the heavenly being to blame.
You see, for the last two thousand years,
She's struggled to comfort—allay people's fears.

"Her hours are frightful; her job's never done.
She's not had a single break. Now she wants one.
With the world so full of sadness and crime,
All guardian angels must work overtime.

"One of them noticed that you might be free.
I know it's unorthodox, but might you be?"
"You can't mean it," I gasped, but his eyes filled with sorrow.
"Please, can't you be an angel tomorrow?

"It's just for one day. See, I have here a list."
I frowned at the thick scroll he held in his fist.
"All right." I took it. "I'll do your bidding."
Then I read the long page and laughed. "Are you kidding?

"Look at all this stuff. There's no earthly way
That I can get it all done in just one day."
But my words simply echoed; the angel was gone.
In the window, I saw the pink touch of dawn.

I rushed to the shower. The room filled with steam.
  I almost convinced myself it was a dream.
    Like a typical morning, I got the kids up,
Made breakfast, signed notebooks, and let out the pup,

Kissed my husband good-bye, got the kids on the bus,
  Walked past the counter, and there the scroll was.
    It glowed with a light I could not ignore,
With a quick huff I grabbed it and shot out the door.

I walked down twelve houses, hit the doorbell, and ran.
From the front yard I heard, "We slept in again!
You can make it to work if you get up this minute!"
Soon I was back at my car and got in it.

I drove a few blocks and screeched to a halt.
Then I called to the man there, "It's not your fault!"
I parked in the lot and raced to the corner
And got there just in time to warn her,

"Hold your child's hand tight." A car swerved as it passed,
But we were all safe, so again, off I dashed.
I rushed around whispering, hugging, and warning
Wondering why I had said "yes" this morning.

At the end of the day, I came home exhausted.
When by my family I was accosted.
"Honey, I don't really mean to be rude.
But what is for dinner?" I suggested fast food.

I ordered, then noticed a mom with a mob
Of young screaming children. "You do a great job."
She stared at me blankly as I took my place
Then a great grin exploded across her whole face.

When at last I collapsed in my bed close to one,
Knowing full well that the list was all done,
I expected some trumpets or heavenly choir,
But I was out cold before it could transpire.

The next morning I waited when the family had gone,
Thinking I'd hear something about what I'd done.
In the silence, I decided to make my own list
Of all that I had to do—with a twist.

N ot only was shopping and cleaning all there,
But I added a few things I thought of with prayer.
I'd drop by two friends I'd not seen in a while,
Share cookies, a compliment, or simply a smile.

Two weeks later, I'd forgotten my angelic visit.
Life had moved on, and time had moved with it.
Although I faced challenges, something had shifted.
Amid all the craziness, I felt uplifted.

As I snuggled in bed and closed my eyes tight,
I was once again shocked by an angel of light.
Only this one was Gladys, of that I was sure,
The angel I'd covered for two weeks before.

Her face beamed with joy. "So you are the one
Who came to my rescue when I was undone.
But that is not why I'm here," she said, glowing.
"I'm so very grateful you kept right on going.

"*S erving and loving and watching for need.*
The difference you've made is great indeed."
"Actually," I said, "it's been easy of late
To serve a bit more because life has been great."

"Perhaps," Gladys said, "with all you've been doing,
Helping us angels in what we're pursuing,
I've had much more time—there's been less to do.
And I've used all those moments I had helping you."

About the Author

After receiving her BA in English from Brigham Young University, Christine married Greg Thackeray and had seven beautiful children—five boys and two girls. During that time, she maintained a love of writing and developed a phonics program used in local private schools. Later she authored several welcome brochures for her hometown, in addition to road shows, Christmas plays, and the odd letter to the editor.

When her youngest son went to kindergarten, she began working as a market analyst, writing hundreds of pages of data. That's when she discovered her interest in publishing and decided to seriously pursue a lifelong dream.

In 2007, Christine's first novel, *Crayon Messages: A Visiting Teaching Adventure* was published. That same year, Christine worked with her sister to coauthor *C. S. Lewis: Latter-day Truths in Narnia*.

Her next novel, *Lipstick Wars: Another Visiting Teaching Adventure* is due to be released later this year. For Christine, writing has become a great gift that fills her days with joy and leaves her evenings available for family. It is like quilting with words.

0 26575 53467 2